CARROT

To Do:
- Eat carrots
- Plant carrots
- Collect carrots
- Eat carrots

CARROT DIARIES

THE COMPLETE GUIDE TO GROWING CARROTS

CARROT RECIPES

AN ODE TO THE CARROT

Carrot desserts

Carrot POETRY

BEST IN SHOW

KEEP CALM AND CARROT ON

PRORERTY OF RABBIT

CARROT

CARROT

CARROT

CARROT

CARROT

CARROT

I CAR

TOO MANY CARROTS

Katy Hudson

CURIOUS FOX
a capstone company—
publishers for children

First published in 2016
by Curious Fox, an imprint of
Capstone Global Library Limited,
264 Banbury Road, Oxford OX2 7DY
Registered company number: 6695582

www.curious-fox.com

Copyright © Katy Hudson 2016

For My Fiancé
– K.H.

The author's moral rights are hereby asserted.
Illustrations by Katy Hudson

All characters in this publication are fictitious
and any resemblance to real persons, living
or dead, is purely coincidental.

ISBN 978 1 78202 415 6

A CIP catalogue for this book is available
from the British Library.

Printed and bound in India.

Rabbit LOVED carrots!

He collected them wherever he went.

Rabbit was proud of his collection
and burrowed it away in his cosy hole.

But Rabbit had a problem. A BIG problem.

He couldn't sleep!

His cosy hole was too crowded to live in.

"I need a place to sleep," Rabbit told Tortoise.

"You could share my house," Tortoise offered.

"It looks cosy and snug," Rabbit said.

"Maybe it's a little TOO snug for two?" suggested Tortoise.

"Not at all," said Rabbit.

"Oh, dear. Well, perhaps we can stay in Bird's nest," said Rabbit.

"My nest is quite small, Rabbit," said Bird.

"I'm sure we will all fit," replied Rabbit.

TOP

8TH

3RD

Rabbit hauled all his carrots up the tree.

"WHOA!" groaned Tortoise
and Bird as the branch wobbled
and swayed . . .

. . . and SNAPPED!

CRASH!

"I'm so sorry, Bird. Now THREE of us don't have a place to sleep," said Rabbit.

"You can sleep in my house," offered Squirrel.

"Oh, thank you, Squirrel! How kind of you," said Rabbit.

"I don't think any more carrots will fit, Rabbit," said Squirrel.

"Just a few more," Rabbit replied.

"Uh-oh," whimpered Tortoise, Bird and Squirrel.

"Now FOUR of us don't have anywhere
to sleep," grumbled Squirrel.

"You can sleep at my house," called Beaver.
"It has plenty of space."

"Great! I can bring even more carrots,"
Rabbit said with a smile.

"But with all your carrots, we can't fit inside,"
said Beaver, a bit bewildered.

Just then, the rain started. Tortoise shivered.
Bird whimpered. Squirrel squeaked.

And Beaver heard a TERRIBLE rumble
as his house collapsed.

"Oh, no! My house!" yelled Beaver.

"Oh, no! My carrots!" cried Rabbit.

"Ahh

hhhhhhhhhh!”

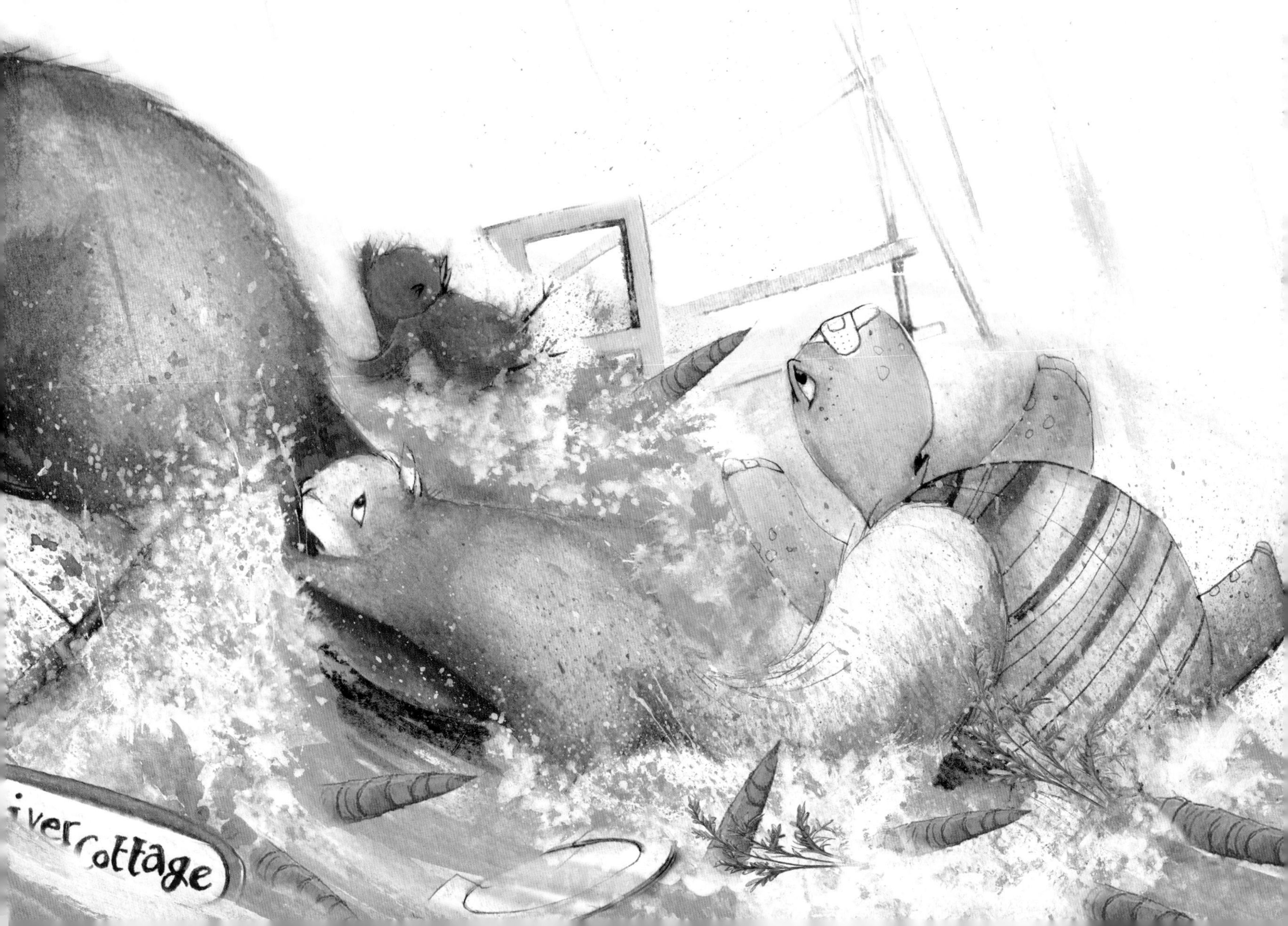

CRASH!

The friends groaned as they
swept up onto the riverbank.

Rabbit felt terrible. His friends were cold, tired and homeless, and it was all his fault.

Even worse, Rabbit still had ALL of his carrots AND his house.

And that's when he realized there was only one thing to do . . .

...Share everything with his friends! After all, carrots weren't for collecting – they were for

PARTY!

SHARING!

And sharing made EVERYTHING better.

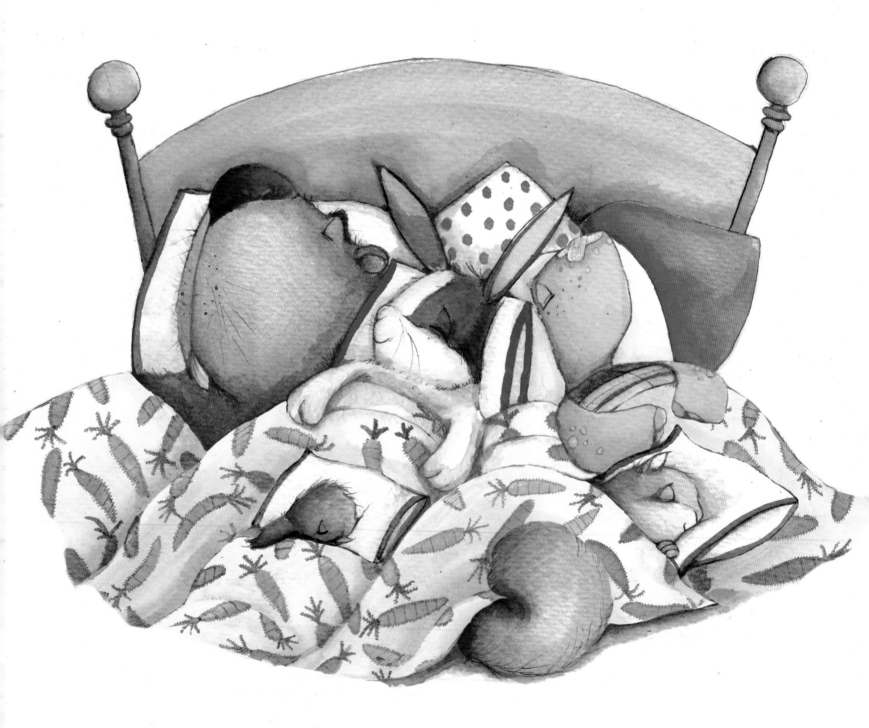